Japanese Fairy Tales

VOLUME 1

Stories by Keisuke Nishimoto
Illustrations by Yoko Imoto

HEIAN

© 1997 Text by Keisuke Nishimoto / Illustrations by Yoko Imoto
Originally published in Japan by Kodansha Ltd.
© 1998 English Edition by Heian International, Inc. USA

Translated by Dianne Ooka
Edited by Charisse Vega, Lisa Melton, and Monique Leahey Sugimoto

First American Edition 1999
99 00 01 02 03 04 05 10 9 8 7 6 5 4 3 2 1

HEIAN INTERNATIONAL, INC.
1815 West 205th Street, Suite #301
Torrance, CA 90501
Web Site : www.heian.com
E-mail: heianemail@heian.com

ISBN: 0-89346-845-2

Web site: www.heian.com
E-mail: heianemail@heian.com

Printed in Hong Kong

Table of Contents

VOLUME 1

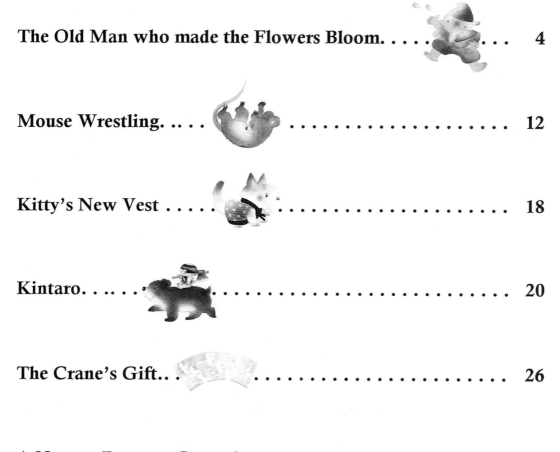

The Old Man who made the Flowers Bloom

Long ago, an old man and old woman lived in the countryside of Japan. One day, as the old woman was washing clothes in the stream near their home, a big wooden box came floating downstream.

"I wonder what that could be," she said puzzled. She pulled it out of the stream and carried it home. When she opened the box, out jumped a lively little puppy!

"Oh, how cute you are!" she cried. "Surely you are a gift from the gods!"

The old couple raised the puppy with tender loving care. It was just like a child to them. The puppy grew bigger day by day and soon was a big, handsome dog.

One day the dog said to the old man, "Please get on my back—and bring a big sack and a hoe."

"Oh no! I'm much too heavy to ride on your back. I could never do that!" said the old man.

"Don't argue—just get on!" insisted the dog.

The old man closed his eyes, and the dog began climbing up the mountainside. Soon he announced, "Here we are!"

The old man opened his eyes and found himself in a grassy meadow. The dog led him to the middle of the field and barked, "Okay...now dig here!"

And guess what! When the old man began to dig, hundreds of gold coins came flying out of the ground!

Surprised, the old man quickly scooped up all of the gold coins and stuffed them into the sack.

He rushed home and called his wife, "Mother, Mother...look at what I've brought you!"

"Oh, my goodness—I've never seen so much money," cried the old woman. And as they were counting the treasure, their greedy old neighbor came to visit.

"Where did you ever find so much money?" asked the neighbor.

The old man told him about what their dog had done.

"Well then...in that case, I'll just have to find me some money, too!" said the greedy old man.

The dog didn't really want to go, but the neighbor cruelly pulled him up to the mountain meadow. When he began to bark, the greedy man began to dig. But instead of the gold coins, out came rocks, broken bowls and slithering snakes.

"You liar!" cried the greedy man. He was so angry that he killed the dog and buried him in the meadow.

When the kind old man realized what had happened, he climbed to the meadow again.

"We should never have let the greedy old man take you away," cried the old man at the dog's grave. Then he noticed a little pine tree that was just beginning to grow and he took it home as a remembrance of his beloved pet. When he planted the tree in his garden, it began to grow very quickly.

Soon the tree was so tall that the old man cut it down. He used the thickest part of the trunk to make a mortar for pounding rice. *And guess what!* When he and his wife began to pound rice, out flew hundreds and hundreds of gold coins!

The greedy neighbor saw this and said, "Hey, I'm using that mortar, too!" He picked up the mortar and carried it home without even waiting for the old man's permission.

But when he and his wife began to pound the rice, out flew rocks, broken bowls and slithering snakes!

"You're not making a fool of me again!" cried the greedy man. He was so angry that he chopped the mortar into little pieces and then burned it to ashes.

"What a terrible thing to do..." mourned the kind old man when he saw what his neighbor had done. He gathered up all of the ashes carefully and carried them home.

9

Just as the old man began to bury the ashes, a sudden gust of wind blew. The ashes scattered here and there. When they landed on the bare trees in the garden, flowers magically began to bloom.

Filled with wonder, the old man began to bury the ashes and went out to an old cherry tree in front of his house. He climbed up into the tree just as a prince and his two servants were passing by. They called out to him, "Hey, old man, what are you doing up there?"

"I'm the number one flower maker in all of Japan!" replied the old man.

So saying, the old man scattered some ashes over the tree. *And guess what!* On this branch...on that branch...on every branch, cherry blossoms began to bloom. Soon the tree was covered with flowers!

The prince was amazed at the sight, and he was so pleased that he gave the old man many fabulous gifts.

Seeing this, the greedy old neighbor scooped up all the ashes he could find and climbed up into the tree outside of his house. He called to the prince, "Hey, hey there, look at me—I'm better than he is!" and he threw the ashes everywhere.

But instead of making any flowers bloom, the wind blew the ashes into the faces of the prince and his servants. The prince was so angry that he sent his servants to pull the old man out of the tree...and they beat him soundly!

Mouse Wrestling

Long ago a very poor old man and old woman lived in Japan. One day when the old man went into the mountains to gather firewood, he heard little voices shouting, "Alley-oop! Alley-oop!

"Who could that be?" wondered the old man, and he moved in the direction of the voices. He came to a clearing and saw two mice wrestling in a ring made of leaves! One mouse was very small and the other was very big. When he looked closely, he saw that the skinny mouse was the mouse who lived at his house, and the other mouse was the fat mouse who lived at the house of their rich neighbor, Mr. Choja.

Choja's mouse was really powerful—when the skinny mouse ran into him, he just bounced off like a feather. He was losing the match, and the old man felt very sorry for the little mouse. When he went home that night, he told his wife about the wrestling match. They decided to use some of their precious rice to make rice cakes for the skinny mouse. The old man left the rice cakes at the front door of his house.

The next day the old man went to the mountains to gather firewood again, he heard the voices shouting, "Alley-oop! Alley-oop!" He hurried to the clearing and found the two mice wrestling, this time in a ring made of acorns.

Today the skinny mouse was much stronger. Suddenly, Choja's fat mouse went flying through the air! The skinny mouse had thrown him out of the ring.

"That's amazing! How did you get so strong?" asked Choja's mouse.

The skinny mouse replied proudly, "I'm stronger because the old man and old woman gave me rice cakes for dinner."

"I see," said Choja's mouse. "Then have them make me some, too!"

"Okay," answered the skinny mouse. "But they are very poor, and they don't have enough rice to make rice cakes for us all the time. If you give them some money, I'm sure they'll be able to buy rice to make rice cakes for you too."

The old man listened to the mice, and that night he and the old woman made rice cakes for both of the mice. The old woman also sewed two little loincloths of red cotton, and the old man left them at the front door together with the rice cakes.

The next morning when they opened the door, both loincloths and rice cakes were gone—and in their place was a shiny gold coin!

Overjoyed at their good fortune, the old man and woman hurried into the mountains. When they arrived at the clearing, they saw the two mice wrestling happily, all dressed up in their red loincloths.

"Alley-oop! Alley-oop!" they shouted. But no matter how hard they tried, neither mouse could beat the other.

The mice looked so funny that the old couple laughed until they cried. From that day on, Choja's mouse brought them a shiny gold coin everyday for their rice cakes. The old man and woman became rich and lived happily ever after!

Kitty's New Vest

Long ago an old man and old woman who had no children were given a little kitten.

"Oh, what a cute little kitten," exclaimed the old woman.

"She sure is cute," agreed her husband.

They loved the kitten and treated it just as they would a child of their own. One day the old man went to town and saw someone selling little vests for children.

"I bet Kitty would be happy to wear one of these," he thought, so he quickly bought one and hurried home.

But when he got home, his wife said, "No matter how cute you think the vest is, Kitty will really look silly in it!"

Kitty, however, climbed into her lap and mewed, "Neow, neow...let me wear it!"

"See," exclaimed the old man. "Kitty can speak Japanese! She's saying *neow*! And in Japanese, *niau* means *it will look nice*!"

"Is that so? All right then, let's see!" said the old lady.

And sure enough, when the old lady put the little vest on Kitty, Kitty looked just wonderful and cuter than ever, mewing *"Neow, I look nice— neow, neow*!"

Kintaro

Long ago, a little boy named Kintaro lived in a cave on Mount Ashigara with his mother. Kintaro was a strong little boy, who played and wrestled happily with his animal friends. One day, after Kintaro had already beaten the deer and the wild boar, the bear bravely stepped forward and declared, "Okay okay... it's my turn now."

"Oomph, oomph!" grunted Kintaro and the bear as they struggled fiercely, each trying to win.

Finally, Kintaro gave a great shout, lifted the bear high in the air and threw him out of the wrestling ring.

"Kintaro won!" cried the monkey who was referee for the match.

"That's it," lamented the bear. "Nobody can beat Kintaro," he said, as he rubbed his sore behind.

Everyday Kintaro wandered through the mountainside. The agile monkey taught him how to climb trees, and the fleet-footed deer showed him how to run along the mountain paths. All of the animals loved strong, good natured Kintaro.

When it rained, the animals would come to play with Kintaro in his cave. There he would use grass and twigs to make toys for them.

Kintaro's mother watched him proudly, and she always prayed to the gods of the mountain, "Please take care of my son and keep him from harm."

When they were out in the forest, Kintaro and his friends gathered many delicious foods. The deer and foxes found ferns and mushrooms; the monkeys and rabbits dug up potatoes; and the squirrels picked acorns and chestnuts. The bear then carried the harvest back to Kintaro's cave.

Thus, even when winter came to the mountains, Kintaro's cave was filled with fruits, nuts and vegetables. Kintaro, his mother, and the animals passed the long days and nights in the cave until, at long last, spring arrived.

One day, Kintaro set out to explore the neighboring mountain. He rode on the bear's back and all the other animals followed.

After a while, they came to a deep ravine.

"Oh, gee...now what'll we do," groaned the animals when they saw the ravine. "Now we'll never get to the other mountain!"

"Don't worry," cried Kintaro. "Leave it to me!"

Kintaro began to push against a big tree growing nearby. The tree began to lean...and lean...and then, boom! It fell right over the top of the ravine and made a perfect bridge to the other side!

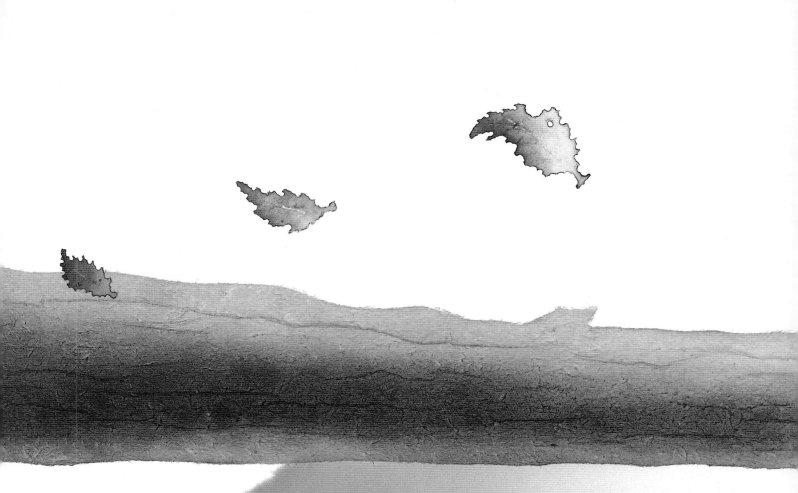

"Fantastic! What a strong boy!" boomed a loud voice.

Kintaro looked around. He saw a great big samurai who had been watching him.

"Hey, young fellow! How would you like to be one of my soldiers?" asked the samurai.

Kintaro was overjoyed to hear this. He gladly left Mount Ashigara and went to live in the capital of Japan. Before long, he became the famous warrior known throughout the land as Kintoki of Sakata.

The Crane's Gift

Long ago there lived a very kind-hearted young man in the Japanese countryside. One day, when he was working in his rice paddy, a beautiful white crane came fluttering down from the sky. Someone had shot the crane with an arrow, and it was stuck in her back.

Murmuring softly to the crane, the young man carefully removed the arrow and cleaned the wound. The crane then flew joyfully into the sky, circling above the young man and crying loudly as if to thank him. She then disappeared into the mountains.

"I'm glad I was able to help that crane," thought the young man, and he worked in the field until late into the starry night.

When he returned home, the young man was surprised to see a lovely girl standing at his front door.

"Please let me be your wife," said the young woman. She was the most beautiful person he had ever seen!

"But...I'm very poor, and I can't possibly support you," said the young man sadly. At that, the young woman handed him a little silk bag.

"This is a rice-producing bag. With this, you never need to worry about having enough food to eat," she said.

And so the young man happily married the beautiful woman. He learned that she was very kind and also a hard worker. Thanks to the magical, mysterious silk bag, they always had rice to eat.

One day, his young wife asked, "Would you build me a shed where I can weave some silk?"

Eager to do whatever he could for his wife, the husband built a weaving shed.

"This is all I ask. Once I enter this shed, I will stay in it for one week. During that time—no matter what—don't ever look inside," said his wife as she went into the weaving shed.

Thereafter, day and night, there came the *thunk, thunk* sound of the shuttle on the loom. On the evening of the seventh day, his wife emerged. She looked pale and weak, but she unfolded the most beautiful piece of silk that the young man had ever seen.

"This is the cloth that I have woven. Please take it to town tomorrow, you should be able to get alot of money for it," she said.

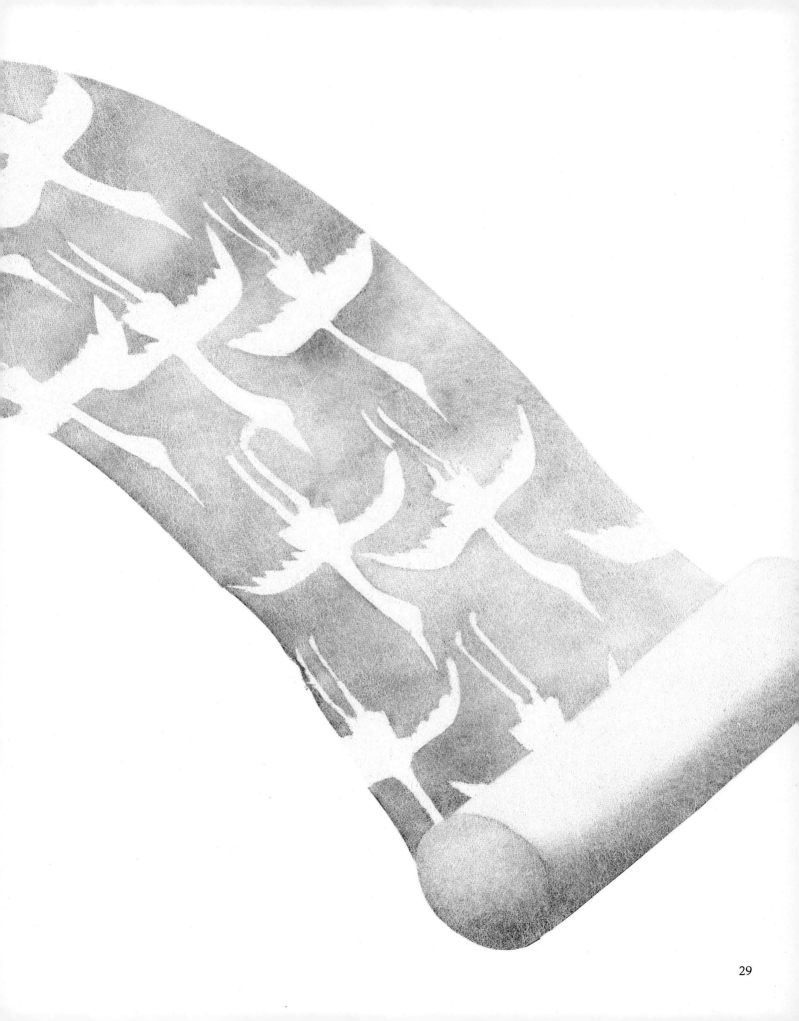

Sure enough, the young man was able to sell the silk for many gold coins the next day. When he joyfully returned home, he again heard *thunk, thunk* coming from the weaving shed.

"Hmmm...I wonder how she weaves that silk, anyway," and filled with curiosity, he peeked through a crack in the front door.

And there, in the weaving shed—instead of his wife—he saw the beautiful white crane! The crane was painfully plucking out her own feathers one by one and weaving them into a beautiful silk fabric.

The husband gasped loudly in surprise. The crane heard him and looked up. She said sadly, "I am the crane that you rescued in the rice paddy. I came back to you and became your wife because you saved my life. But now that you've broken your promise and have seen me, I can no longer stay here with you."

And so saying, she flew away—circling high up into the sky, crying soft farewells.

A NOTE TO PARENTS:
Capturing a Child's Imagination

Children are just full of curiosity. They're always looking about expectantly, wanting to discover new things. The more they learn, the wider their eyes open to find what interests them.

A child's interest in books begin with wordless picture books, then turns to picture books with stories. Though some children may read and interpret these storybooks on their own, most must rely on an adult to help read and interpret the stories for them. During this important period of development, it is critical for children to have stories read aloud to them by an adult. A child's mother and father are the adults who are the closest and most dear to the child. Indeed, hearing the loving voice of a mother or father telling (and retelling) a story can become one of the child's most reassuring memories. In addition, by reading stories aloud, parents enrich their child's imagination. Just as food provides nutrition for the child's growing body, the interchange between child and parent during storytelling can be a nutrient for the mind and soul.

The collection of stories in this volume include some of Japan's most cherished tales. As with all fables and legends, it isn't clear where, by whom, or even when these stories were composed. Most likely, the tales grew out of the daily lives of our ancestors and from generation to generation, were passed from parent to child. What is clear about the fairy tales, however, is their value. Whose imagination wouldn't be captivated by a magical white crane, mice wrestling, Japan's best flower maker, and other stories of the fantastic? But the *Japanese Fairy Tales* are more than just entertaining; they also address some of life's enduring themes: How to live a good, kind life; how to achieve happiness; and the price to be paid for cruelty, greediness, and cowardice. Through these tales, then, and through the humorous way in which they are told, children learn human virtue and traditional wisdom.

Keisuke Nishimoto, Professor
Showa Woman's College
Tokyo, Japan